UP, UP, AND AWAY

A Follett JUST Beginning-To-Read Book

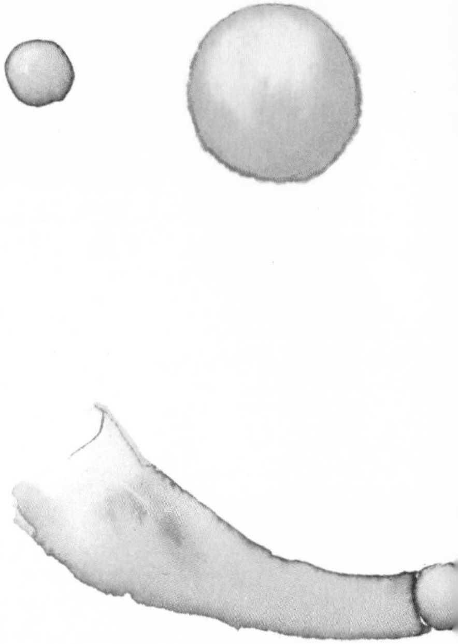